The Berenstain Bears

HOSPITAL FRIENDS

Our hospital friends
take good care of us all.
Let's visit the hospital
and pay them a call!

Mike Berenstain

Based on the characters created by Stan and Jan Berenstain

Medical Consultant: Laura K. Diaz, MD,
The Children's Hospital of Philadelphia, Department of Anesthesiology and Critical Care Medicine

Our sincere thanks to The Children's Hospital of Philadelphia
for their generous cooperation in the creation of this book

HARPER FESTIVAL
An Imprint of HarperCollinsPublishers

Library of Congress catalog card number: 2014952917 • ISBN 978-0-06-207541-3
16 17 18 19 CWM 10 9 8 7 6 5 4   • ❖ • First Edition

The Bear family was visiting the Bear Country Hospital. Their cousin Fred had just had his tonsils taken out. They were bringing him a card and a balloon that said "Get well soon!" On the way to his room, they passed busy doctors, nurses, and other hospital workers.

Cousin Fred was sitting up in bed eating a bowl of ice cream. Aunt Min was with him. She had a bed in the corner in case she needed to stay overnight.

"Hiya, Fred!" said Brother and Sister. "How are you feeling?"

"Hi," said Fred. His voice was soft and raspy. "My throat hurts. That's why I'm eating this. It's the only thing that feels good on my throat."

"You get ice cream here?" said Brother. "I want to stay in the hospital, too!"

"I don't know if you can stay," said a voice behind them. "But I'll give you a tour."

It was Dr. Gert Grizzly, their family doctor. She was there to check on Cousin Fred.

"Can we really have a tour, Dr. Grizzly?" asked Sister.

"Of course!" said the doctor. "This would be a good time for you to learn all about the hospital."

Dr. Grizzly looked
Cousin Fred over.
    "You're doing fine,
Fred," she said. "I think
you'll be able to go home
today."
    "Hooray," whispered
Fred and went back to his ice
cream.
    "Now let's get started," said
Dr. Grizzly, as they waved good-bye
to Cousin Fred and Aunt Min.

"This part of the hospital is where cubs stay," explained Dr. Grizzly. "We try to make them comfortable. Their parents can stay with them, and there are books, games, toys, and TV. There's plenty of good food—usually more than just ice cream.

"Special workers play with the cubs, read to them, and help them learn. There are even artists and musicians who teach cubs how to paint and play instruments."

"That looks like fun!" said Sister. Brother and Honey nodded.

"Hello, Bonnie," said Dr. Grizzly to a cub with a cast on her leg.

"Good morning, Dr. Grizzly," said Bonnie.

"Bonnie here has a broken bone in her leg," Dr. Grizzly explained.

"May we sign your cast?" asked Sister.

"Sure!" said Bonnie, grinning.

They signed her cast, and Honey drew a heart on it.

"Bonnie and her friends are going to PT—physical therapy," said Dr. Grizzly. "That's where they go to get the special exercise they need."

The Bear family followed Bonnie to PT and watched cubs working on exercise machines and doing other activities to help them grow strong and well.

"When someone has a broken bone, like Bonnie," said Dr. Grizzly, "we often take X-rays to learn more about it."

"What are X-rays?" asked Brother.

"You can see for yourself," said Dr. Grizzly, showing them. There was a window onto a room with a big machine. A patient's leg was propped under it. A doctor was holding pictures from the machine up to a light. You could actually see the patient's bones right in the pictures!

"Wow!" said Sister.

"Cool!" said Brother.

"COOL!" said Honey.

"X-rays are one way we learn about a patient," said Dr. Grizzly. "But first we do exams and other things to decide what needs to be done. Sometimes there needs to be an operation."

"Like when Cousin Fred had his tonsils taken out?" asked Sister.

"That's right!" said Dr. Grizzly. "Let's see what happens before an operation."

They went to a room where nurses and doctors were getting patients ready for operations. A cub was there with her mom and dad. Doctors were giving her medicine to make her comfortable and drowsy. They explained about all the other things they would do to keep her safe and to make sure nothing felt bad.

CHART

The Bear family saw doctors and nurses washing their hands. They wore gowns, hats, and rubber gloves, and were putting masks over their noses and mouths.

"Everyone who works with patients in an operation has to wash carefully to clean away germs," explained Dr. Grizzly.

"Why are they wearing masks and all that other stuff?" asked Sister.

"That's to protect against germs, too," said Dr. Grizzly. "Even after washing, we all have germs that can make a patient sick."

"Where do patients go after an operation?" asked Brother.

"To recovery," said Dr. Grizzly taking them into a room where more patients were being cared for. Dr. Grizzly pointed out a plastic bag with tubes attached.

"That's an IV," she said. "It gives patients liquids to keep them healthy."

Some of the patients were asleep. One cub was just waking up.
"Were they taking naps?" asked Sister.
"Not exactly," said Dr. Grizzly. "When cubs have an operation, there are doctors and nurses who help them fall asleep and stay safe until they wake up with their moms and dads."

"When someone comes to the hospital," asked Brother, "where do they go first?"

"Often, right to the Emergency Department—the ED," said Dr. Grizzly. "That's the last stop on our tour."

They passed through a waiting area for families of patients who had just arrived and greeted a nurse at a desk.

"This is Nurse Brown," said Dr. Grizzly. "She finds out all about the patients when they first come in."

"Most of the patients are sent to an exam room," said Nurse Brown. "Would you like to see one?"

She took them to a row of small rooms with curtains. They saw a doctor listening to a cub's breathing while a nurse took his temperature and checked his heart.

"After patients are examined," explained Nurse Brown, "they sometimes go for more tests or treatment."

"How do all these patients get to the hospital, anyway?" asked Sister.

"When folks need to go to the hospital in a hurry," said Nurse Brown, taking them outside, "an ambulance will rush them right here. Emergency workers can even give care and medicine in the ambulance while it's on its way."

BEAR COUNTRY HOSPITAL

"Sometimes," Dr. Grizzly told them, "patients are brought even faster or from far away in a special helicopter that lands right on the hospital roof."

"WOW!" said the cubs.

"Oh my!" said Mama, holding her hat in the breeze.

"WOW!" said Papa.

"Now our hospital tour is done," said Dr. Grizzly. "I hope you enjoyed learning about the hospital as much as I enjoyed showing it to you."

"Yes, we did!" said the Bear family. "Thank you, Dr. Grizzly!"

"Thank you, indeed, doctor," said Mama. "We've met so many new friends here today—the doctors, the nurses, and everyone else who works hard to make the hospital a special place. And we've learned that when we come to the hospital, our hospital friends will take good care of us all!"